THIS **Elephant & Piggie** BOOK
BELONGS TO:

_____

_____

_____

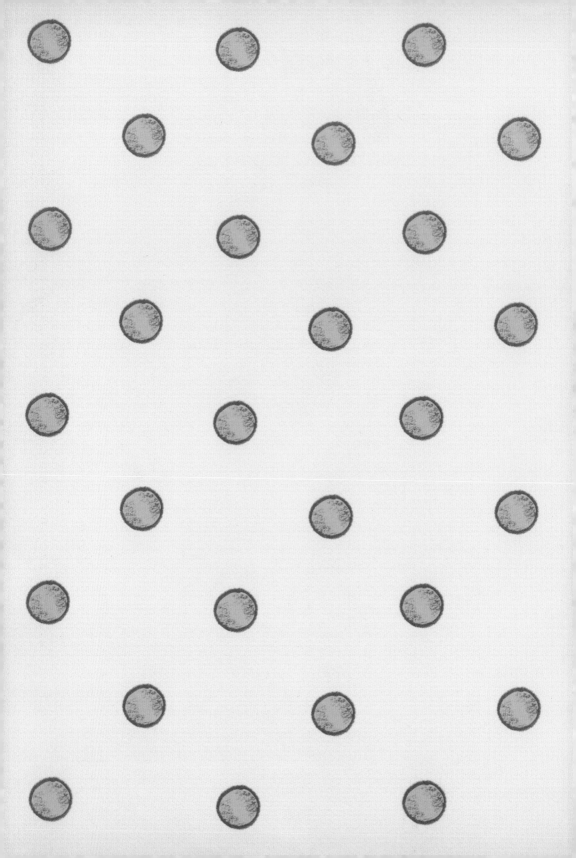

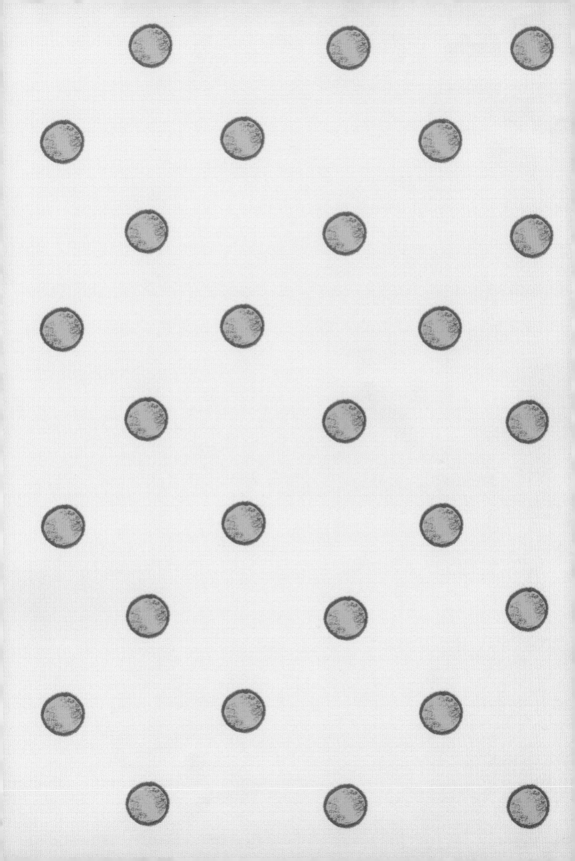

For Max, Sam, Amanda and Irving

Watch Me Throw the Ball!

Mo Willems

WALKER BOOKS
AND SUBSIDIARIES
LONDON · BOSTON · SYDNEY · AUCKLAND

An Elephant & Piggie Book

You found my ball!

This is
your ball?

I am very good
at throwing.

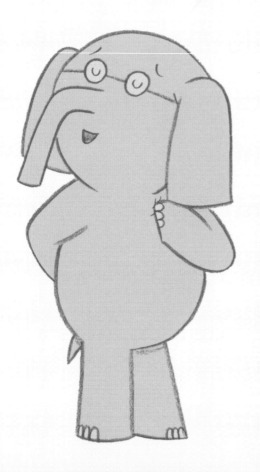

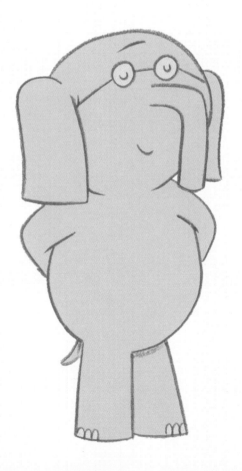

You want to throw my ball?

Yes!

Do you know the secret
to throwing?

Throwing this ball
is not easy!

I worked very hard to learn how to throw a ball.

Got it.

May I
try now?

Yes.

Maybe one day you can throw like me. But—

ZIP!

22

23

THE PIG IS

THROWING!

FLING!

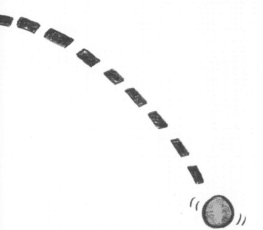

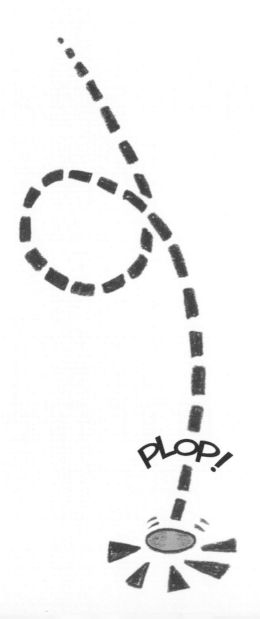

Call me
"Super Pig"!

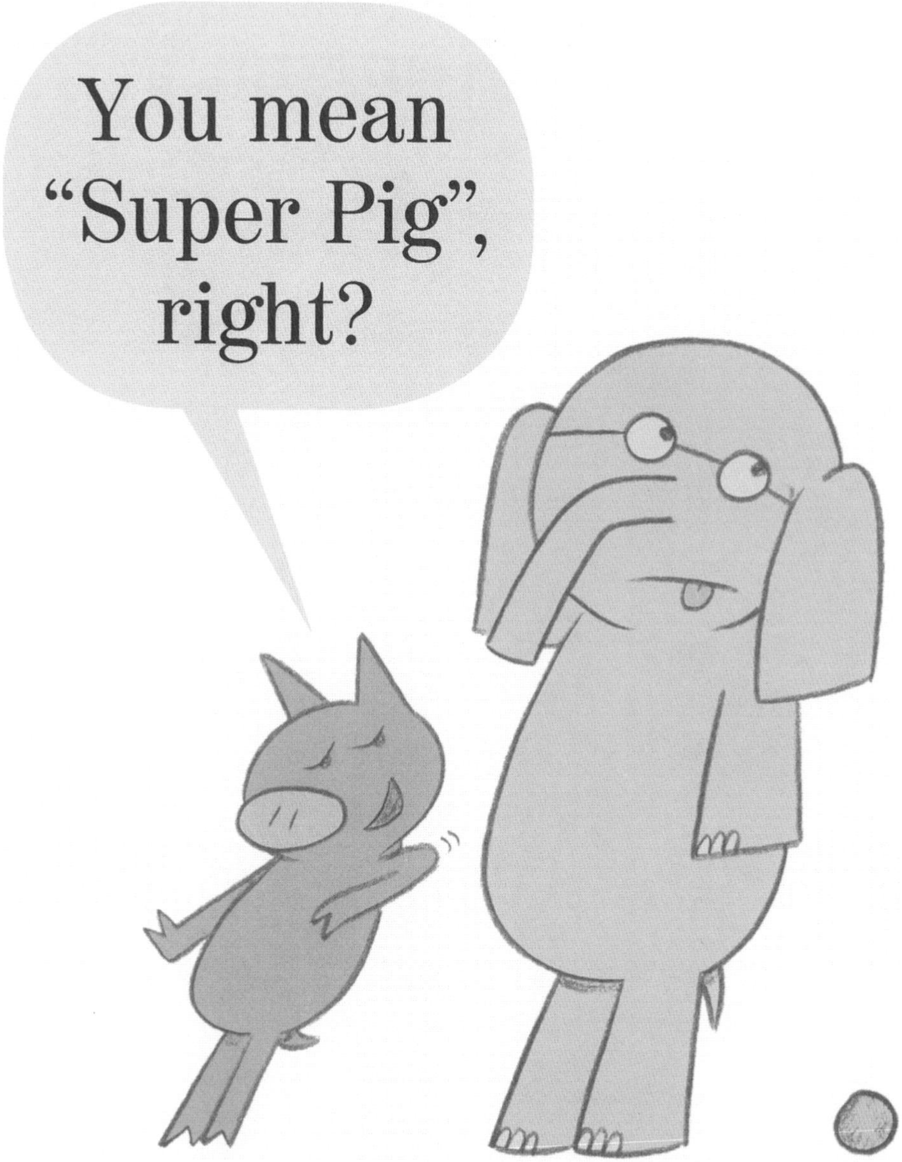
You mean “Super Pig”, right?

41

The ball flew behind you and fell here!

Not very far at all...

But I
had fun!

FLING!

56

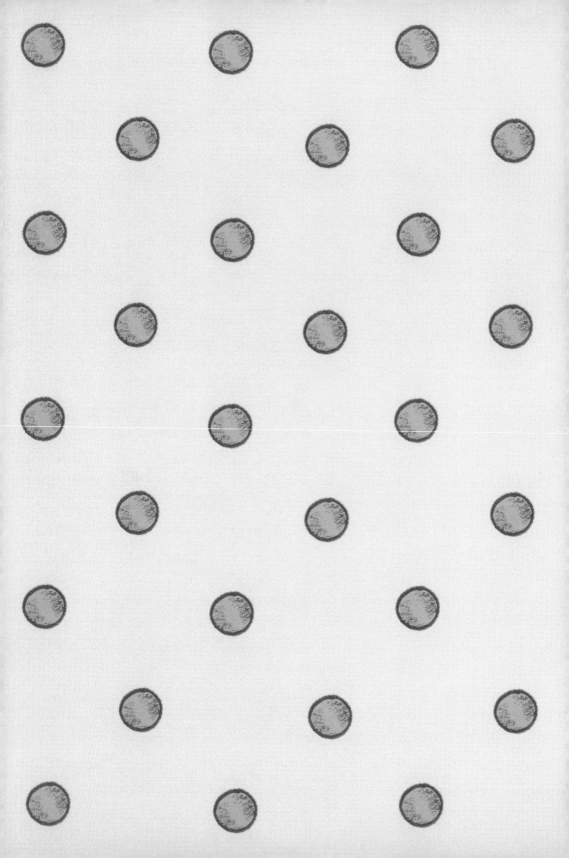

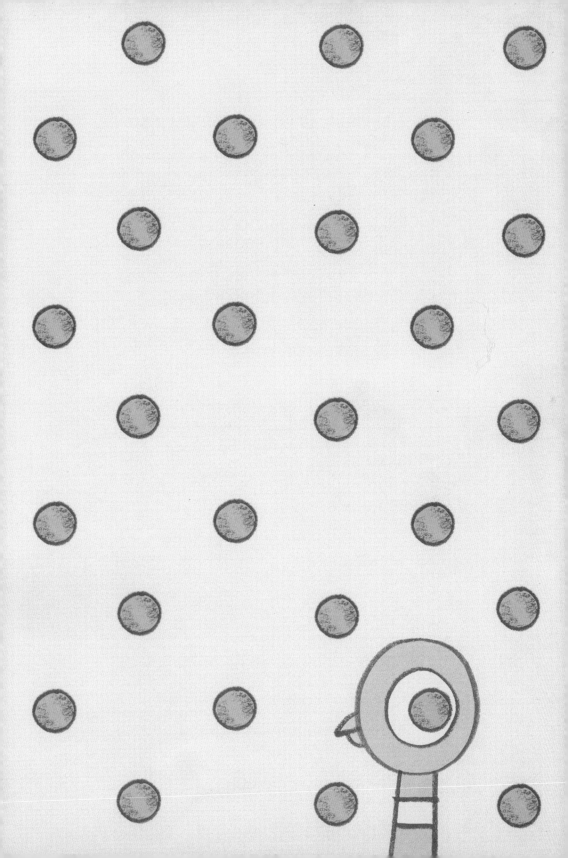

Mo Willems is the renowned author of many award-winning books, including the Caldecott Honor winners *Don't Let the Pigeon Drive the Bus!*, *Knuffle Bunny* and *Knuffle Bunny Too*. His other groundbreaking picture books include *Knuffle Bunny Free, Leonardo, the Terrible Monster* and *Edwina: The Dinosaur Who Didn't Know She Was Extinct*. Before making picture books, Mo was a writer and animator on Sesame Street, where he won six Emmys. Mo lives with his family in Massachusetts, USA.

Visit him online at **www.mowillems.com** and **www.GoMo.net**

This is a work of fiction. Names, characters, places and incidents are either the product of the author's imagination or, if real, used fictitiously.

First published in Great Britain 2009 by Walker Books Ltd
87 Vauxhall Walk, London SE11 5HJ

First published in the United States by Hyperion Books for Children
British publication rights arranged with Sheldon Fogelman Agency, Inc.

This edition published 2013

2 4 6 8 10 9 7 5 3

© 2008, 2013 Mo Willems

The right of Mo Willems to be identified as author and illustrator of this work has been asserted by him in accordance with the Copyright, Designs and Patents Act 1988

This book has been typeset in Century 725 and Grilled Cheese

Printed in South China

British Library Cataloguing in Publication Data:
a catalogue record for this book is available from the British Library

ISBN 978-1-4063-4827-9

www.walker.co.uk